CIARA AND THE UNICORN'S FARM FIASCO

BY ELAINE HENEY

Books for kids

My sister is a unicorn series
Ciara & the Unicorn's New York Adventure
Ciara & the Unicorn's Farm Fiasco

For adults

Equine Listenology Guide
Equine Listenology Workbook
Equine Listenology Journal
Equine Listenology Diary
Horse Anatomy Coloring Book
Ozzie, the Story of a Young Horse
Conversations with the Horse
The Horse Riders Training Journal

Online horse courses for adults:

www.greyponyfilms.com

iPhone & Android Horse Apps:

www.horsestridesapp.com
www.rideableapp.com
www.dressagehero.com
www.greyponyfilms.com

FOR CLODAGH & CIARA
& EVERYONE WHO BELIEVES IN
UNICORNS & MAGIC

THIS BOOK BELONGS TO:

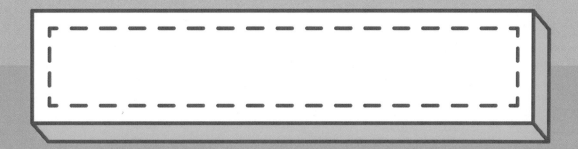

I'm Ciara and my sister is Tilly the unicorn. We're off to visit our grandparents on the farm.

Hurry up Tilly, we're going to be late. I better not forget my wellies!

I love the countryside. There are so many animals and it's so peaceful.... OMG that radio is so loud. I guess everyone knows we're on the way now!

Nana! Papa! We're here!

'Tilly & Ciara it's great to see you.
We have lots of fun lined up. Papa has
lots of jobs on the farm for you.
Tilly, are you hungry already?'

'Tilly & Ciara, I'm so glad you're here' said Papa. 'I need help to muck out the horse's stables.'

OK Papa. Hey Tilly, did you just do a poo?

'What goes in must come out!' says Tilly.

'Oh no, the sheep have got out again.
They keep jumping the wall' said Papa

The sheep are scattered everywhere. But then something strange starts to happen...

'How did you do that?' said Ciara.
'Just call me the sheep whisperer'
said Tilly

Tilly, what did you do? You're so muddy!

'It's my new skincare routine' said Tilly. 'All the celebrities are doing it'.

'Great', said Ciara, 'I want to do it too!' Then Nana walks out the door and sees the mess... oh oh!

And while you're at it, you can help me pick some apples. I want to make a delicious apple pie for our tea.'

Papa your tractor is so cool. Can we go for a spin? Hurry up Tilly, we're going to be farmers! Vroom vroom here we go!

It's lunch time so we need to feed the animals. The horses get an apple. The chickens get fruit & veg and...

What a mess. Now we need to tidy the yard. I've got my pink wheelbarrow ready.

Tilly, where are you?

Wake up Tilly! You fell asleep in the hay shed. Do you know that hay is made from grass? You cut the grass in the summer and then in the winter, our cattle & horses can eat the hay when the grass is gone.

'I'm making jam, but I need to get some blackberries. Can you find some blackberries for me, Ciara & Tilly?' said Nana. 'You'll see them in the hedges.,. But mind the prickly briars.

I've found them Tilly, over here!

But don't walk through the nettles or you'll get stung!

I'm so happy we made it back in one piece. Nana & Papa, this was our best holiday ever. Tilly & I want to be farmers when we grow up too.

READ MORE!

ENJOY THE ENTIRE CIARA + TILLY THE UNICORN BOOK SERIES

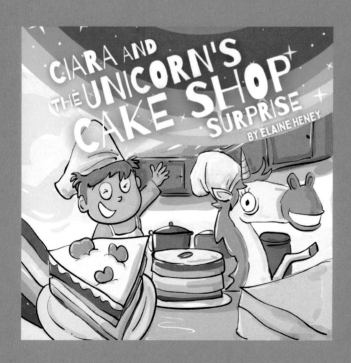

THANK YOU FOR READING THIS BOOK. IF YOU ENJOYED THIS BOOK PLEASE LEAVE A REVIEW!

MORE BOOKS IN THIS UNICORN SERIES ARE WAITING FOR YOU!